Zachary's Ball

Matt Tavares

CANDLEWICK PRESS

To Barbara Gagel

The publisher gratefully acknowledges that references to Fenway Park, along with the Boston Red Sox name, uniform, likeness, and logos, are used by permission of the Boston Red Sox.

AUTHOR'S NOTE

Fenway Park first opened its gates on April 20, 1912. Twenty-seven thousand fans filed into the brand-new ballpark and waited through two rain delays to cheer on the Red Sox as they battled their rivals, the New York Highlanders (who later changed their name to the Yankees). The Sox won that day, 7–6 in 11 innings.

The old ballpark has changed quite a bit since that first game. In 1934, after a fire destroyed much of the original structure, the wooden grandstands were replaced with concrete and steel. Bullpens were installed in front of the right-field bleachers in 1940. And the wall in left field, which stands at a towering 37 feet 3 inches high, was painted green in 1947, giving it its famous nickname, the Green Monster.

As Fenway Park continues to evolve, one thing remains the same as it was on that rainy day back in 1912. Season after season, game after game, baseball fans flock to Fenway to root for their team. It's become a tradition, passed down from generation to generation. I remember going to Fenway with my dad when I was a kid, sitting in the left-field grandstand, wearing my baseball glove, always ready for a foul ball. I remember the thrill of taking my daughters to their first game and introducing them to this special place.

When Fenway Park opened, there were no highways, no computers, no retractable-dome stadiums, no artificial turf, and no multimillion-dollar baseball players. But with all that's changed in one hundred years, Fenway Park is still there, a shrine to baseball's glorious past and a place where family, friends, and complete strangers come together to share stories, watch the game, and maybe even catch a foul ball.

I had never been inside a ballpark until that day. Everything felt so close to me—the outfield fence, the players warming up, even the man who watered the field. I was jealous of him because he got to walk on the same grass as Buck Spoonwell and all the other heroes my father talked about so often.

I remember everybody clapping and hollering when Boston came up to bat.

Hundreds of people in the bleachers chanted in unison, "Let's go, Sox! Let's go, Sox!"

Buck Spoonwell was up first. "Hit a home run, Buck!" my father shouted.

"Let's go, Buck!" I yelled as loud as I could.

On the first pitch, Buck took a mighty swing. But he did not hit a home run. Instead, he popped the ball straight up into the sky. The crowd groaned.

But then, suddenly, the wind picked up and carried the ball right toward us.

My father stood up. So did all the other grownups. I stood up too, even though I was too little to catch the ball. Once all the jumping and yelling stopped, my father sat down, and with a big smile, he held in front of me a beautiful white baseball.

As he handed me the ball, something unbelievable happened.

All of a sudden, I was no longer sitting with my father. I was standing on the pitcher's mound, dressed in a Red Sox uniform.

"One more strike and we win, kid," said Skip Johnson, the manager, as he handed me the ball and returned to the dugout.

I looked at the catcher, crouched down behind the plate, waiting for my pitch. He gave me some sort of sign, but I didn't know what it meant, so I just reared back and threw the ball as hard as I could. The hitter swung as hard as he could, but the ball whizzed past him. Strike three. The Sox win!

The catcher ran out to the mound to give me the game ball. As he handed it to me, suddenly I was back in the stands with my father. It seemed as though no time had passed.

"Dad!" I exclaimed. "This baseball is magic!"

My father smiled. "They're all magic," he said.

I wrote my name on the baseball as soon as I got home that day. That night, I took my ball to bed with me, and each night, from then on, I dreamed about baseball.

One night, I was standing in left field at Fenway Park when New York's best hitter blasted a deep fly ball right toward me. I ran as fast as I could and dove for it, feeling the smack of the ball in my glove as I skidded across the outfield grass.

Another night, I struck out the final batter in the seventh game of the World Series. My teammates all ran out to the mound and held me above their shoulders while thousands of Red Sox fans stormed the field.

Then, one day, my baseball was gone. I looked in the drawer in my desk where I usually kept it. I looked all over my room. For weeks, I looked everywhere. But it was nowhere to be found.

A few months passed, and finally, I gave up.

I still dreamed of baseball, though. And every summer, I spent my Saturday afternoons at the ballpark, rooting for Boston . . .

. . . always hoping that another ball might come my way.

Years later, I was taking a walk in Boston down by the ballpark. The heat was unbearable, so I stopped to rest in a tiny spot of shade. I gazed up at the big wall in front of me. I heard the sound of cheering fans from inside the park.

Just then, out of the sky came a glowing white baseball — a towering home run, hit over the wall. I reached up and it fell gracefully into my outstretched hands. As I spun the dusty ball around, I thought I saw two faded words, written in a child's handwriting —

Zachary's
Ball

Quickly, I tried to brush the dust away so I could read it more clearly. But as the dust vanished into the air, so did the words.

Holding my new baseball, I thought back to the day when my father took me to my first game. I remembered the gift he had given me. Now, I had caught a ball myself—I couldn't wait to tell him.

As I turned to head home, I noticed a young girl holding her father's hand. She was staring at my baseball.

I placed the ball in her hands.

A moment later, she exclaimed, "This baseball is magic!"

"I know," I answered. "They're all magic."